MAXIMILIAN P. MOUSE, TIME TRAVELER

A BRAVE NEW MOUSE

ELLIS ISLAND APPROVED IMMIGRANT

magic
Wagon

BOOK 5

Philip M. Horender • Guy Wolek

visit us at www.abdopublishing.com

To Erin and MoJo – the best part of each day—PMH

Published by Magic Wagon, a division of the ABDO Group, PO Box 398166, Minneapolis, Minnesota 55439. Copyright © 2014 by Abdo Consulting Group, Inc. International copyrights reserved in all countries. All rights reserved. No part of this book may be reproduced in any form without written permission from the publisher.

Calico Chapter Books™ is a trademark and logo of Magic Wagon.

Printed in the United States of America, Melrose Park, Illinois.
052013
092013
 This book contains at least 10% recycled materials.

Text by Philip M. Horender
Illustrations by Guy Wolek
Edited by Stephanie Hedlund and Rochelle Baltzer
Cover and interior design by Neil Klinepier

Library of Congress Cataloging-in-Publication Data

Horender, Philip M.
  A brave new mouse : Ellis Island approved immigrant / by Philip M. Horender ; illustrated by Guy Wolek.
    p. cm. -- (Maximilian P. Mouse, time traveler ; bk. 5)
  Summary: Maximilian lands on a ship of Irish immigrants bound for Ellis Island, where he meets a young girl named Ashling who tells her family's story and smuggles him through immigration, as well as a friendly pelican that takes him on a flight around New York Harbor in search of his damaged time machine.
  ISBN 978-1-61641-961-5
1. Mice--Juvenile fiction. 2. Pelicans--Juvenile fiction. 3. Time travel--Juvenile fiction. 4. Immigrants--United States--Juvenile fiction. 5. Ellis Island (N.J. and N.Y.)--History--Juvenile fiction. 6. New York (N.Y.)--History--20th century--Juvenile fiction. [1. Mice--Fiction. 2. Pelicans--Fiction. 3. Time travel--Fiction. 4. Adventure and adventurers--Fiction. 5. Immigrants--United States--Fiction. 6. Ellis Island (N.J. and N.Y.)--History--Fiction. 7. New York (N.Y.)--History--20th century--Fiction.] I. Wolek, Guy, ill. II. Title.
  PZ7.H78087Br 2013
  813.6--dc23   2012050865

TABLE OF CONTENTS

Chapter 1: Failed Again. 4
Chapter 2: Frozen 7
Chapter 3: Safe and Sound 13
Chapter 4: A Daring Mission 16
Chapter 5: Ashling 22
Chapter 6: A Sad Story 27
Chapter 7: A Bright Hope. 31
Chapter 8: Follow Directions. 37
Chapter 9: Lady Liberty 41
Chapter 10: We Made It!. 48
Chapter 11: I'll Do Anything. 57
Chapter 12: New Dangers 62
Chapter 13: Give Me Your Tired 66
Chapter 14: Nearly Through 71
Chapter 15: Gone! 75
Chapter 16: A New Friend 81
Chapter 17: Faster 85
Chapter 18: An Amazing Ride 91
Chapter 19: Smooth Landing. 96
Chapter 20: Time to Write 100
Chapter 21: Another Try. 103
About Ellis Island. 106
Glossary 108
About the Author. 112

Chapter 1:
FAILED AGAIN

Maximilian could not believe it. The feeling he had now was most definitely that of being on water. But it wasn't the calm, slow-moving tides of the Mississippi River. The inside of this ship was nothing like the beautifully crafted ship he had left back in 1875.

The time machine had failed again. Maximilian was just as disappointed and frustrated as the previous times. But, he did not have time to **wallow**.

Maximilian was on a mission to save his home in Tanner's Glen. When he learned that Farmer Tanner was being foreclosed on, he knew he had to do something as mouse of the house. He had met Nathaniel Chipmunk III and borrowed Nathaniel's time machine.

Besides the Mississippi River in 1875, the time machine had taken Maximilian back in time to Boston in 1773, Gettysburg in 1863, and the Utah Territory in 1869.

What he thought must be another rather large wave rocked the boat. Maximilian's stomach dropped, a feeling he was not at all fond of.

Eyeing a nearby crate, Maximilian scurried up it. He used the wooden hatches like a ladder. He climbed and climbed until he reached the top. What he saw next was absolutely **heart-wrenching**.

The ship was carrying hundreds, maybe thousands, of people. They were all tightly pressed next to one another. Maximilian saw men, women, and children of all ages sitting on top of one another.

These were not the wealthy passengers of a fine, Southern paddleboat. These people looked scared, tired, and **downtrodden**.

Maximilian climbed back down from the crate. He nearly slipped on more than one occasion, rattled from what he had just seen.

He made his way through the boxes and bags and back to the time machine. He would wait the day out inside it if he needed to. At least there he felt safe.

As he turned the corner of the last crate, he neared the time machine. Maximilian watched in horror as the time machine swayed to one side with the next lurch of the boat.

The time machine teetered unsteadily for a brief moment and then tipped over with a loud crash.

Chapter 2:
FROZEN

Maximilian was horrified by the sight of the time machine lying on its side. The blood slowly drained from his face. Before he could fully understand what had happened, the boat rolled again.

The egg-shaped time machine rolled back to its normal position. Maximilian jumped into action. He grabbed a nearby leather luggage strap and ran two quick laps around the time machine. He tightened the belt as much as he could. Then, he fastened it and breathed an uneasy sigh of relief.

Maximilian began to carefully examine the time machine. The acorn shell was strong. But he almost immediately saw a long, clean crack down the left side. The crack did not appear to be very deep. He hoped it proved to be nothing.

Without warning, the boat rode over another large wave. The time machine, securely fastened to the luggage, did not budge.

A large wooden trunk with metal buckles rested next to Maximilian. It must have been fairly heavy because when the ship turned violently, the trunk stood firm.

This chest must have belonged to an owner who had endured much in order to be on this boat. Its straps were worn and its finish was faded. Boldly stamped on the side beneath the key lock was a bright red seal.

Maximilian was still feeling the effects of the time machine's spinning. He braced himself against the trunk to read:

From: Dublin, Ireland
To: New York City, U.S.A.
October 9, 1920
General Fare Paid in Full

Maximilian felt as though he was being toyed with. The month and day were close to the ones he had set into the time machine's panel. But the year was off.

He slammed his paw against the trunk in frustration. He had landed less than twenty minutes ago and had already found himself in a scary situation. The time machine was damaged and he was no closer to Tanner's Glen.

Before he could vent any more, his sensitive ears picked up something. He paused to determine where the sound was coming from. Carefully climbing between two crates and over a box of supplies, Maximilian found the source of the noise. He saw a girl sobbing.

Maximilian watched quietly from a safe distance. The girl wore a long, brown dress with ankle-high leather shoes. Her dress was simple and plain. It was nowhere near as fancy as the dresses Maximilian had seen on the Mississippi steamship or even in Silver Springs.

The girl's red hair was in a long ponytail. When she removed her hands from her face, she exposed rose-colored cheeks and fair skin.

The girl's eyes were swollen from crying. A few stray tears still ran down her face. She removed a handkerchief from her side pocket and dabbed under her eyes. Maximilian thought the girl was eleven or twelve. Although he was sure she had been through more than most children her age.

Maximilian knew nothing about this girl. He wondered why she would be this emotional. At the same time, he felt for her. On more than one occasion on his trip, he had been in her situation.

The girl dried her eyes some more. She sat on a crate labeled Oslo. Maximilian wondered if that was the name of a place or a family.

Maximilian navigated his way around a number of boxes to get closer to the girl. From only a few yards away, he saw that she had the most beautiful green eyes he had ever seen.

Looking over her shoulder, she glanced back at the other passengers crowded into the vessel. Maximilian followed her gaze to a middle-aged couple with a boy no older than five. Like the rest of the families huddled in the ship, they looked tired and scared.

The man looked as though he had not slept. But, he had a reassuring arm wrapped around his wife.

Maximilian looked back at the girl. She now played with her handkerchief nervously. He could see her pain.

"Who are all these people?" Maximilian wondered aloud. He was not quite sure how he should feel. One thing was for sure, he was stuck here for at least twenty-four hours. Hopefully no longer than that, considering the crack in the time machine.

The girl gathered herself and prepared to return to her family. Just then, something made Maximilian freeze. Fear pulsed through his veins.

Just when the girl straightened her legs and got to her feet, Maximilian's watch chimed its familiar chord. His watch's hymn sang softly from inside his pocket. The timing could not have been worse.

The girl stopped and looked directly at Maximilian. He tried to move, but his muscles stood rigid. His hiding spot had been revealed. Those striking green eyes now lay squarely on him.

Chapter 3:
SAFE AND SOUND

Maximilian wanted to run. His heart pounded and his body shook. He willed his legs to carry him back to the time machine or into a nearby crate. But, he stood rooted to the ground like a tree.

The young girl's expression changed. Her eyes brightened and her face relaxed. She peered at him as though she had never seen a mouse before in her life. She touched her finger to her lips and blinked twice.

"What a **dapper** little mouse," she said, leaning closer to him. "What a handsome fellow indeed."

Maximilian's eyes were scanning from one side of the boat to the other. He could take no chances with a human. He had heard stories about animals who got caught and then spent a life trapped in a cage. They were forced to live out their remaining days as a pet. No, he could not afford to take any chances with a human, regardless of how sweet or innocent it appeared.

Finally, Maximilian convinced his legs to carry him away. He sprinted through the wooden slats of a crate full of potatoes and turnips. He squirmed his way to the center of the crate and cautiously peered out. The girl was looking for him. She seemed puzzled as to why he had left when she had paid him such a nice **compliment**.

The girl folded her handkerchief and placed it back in her pocket. She got to her feet and slowly returned to her family.

Maximilian felt relieved and safe. But part of him felt guilty as well. The sight of him had provided a welcome distraction for the girl. Still, Maximilian simply could not take any chances that the girl might have had other plans for him. He fixed his shirt, straightened his coat, and walked back to the time machine.

The waters had calmed and the violent rocking of the boat had stopped. Maximilian looked around. He decided that the situation might be worse than he had originally thought.

Maximilian climbed into the time machine and relocked the hatch. He hoped the next twenty-three hours went by quickly.

Chapter 4:
A DARING MISSION

Despite the close quarters, Maximilian felt safe inside the time machine. It reminded him of home and the promise of a safe return to Tanner's Glen.

It was warm inside the time machine and Maximilian removed his coat. His eyelids grew heavy and he slowly fell asleep.

A lazy summer day in Tanner's Glen typically began with a walk along the banks of the creek. Maximilian could feel the cold, spring water teasing his toes as he walked. The air smelled of wild violets and blooming daisies.

His mother would be back at the oak tending to her garden. His sister Sally would be chasing butterflies.

Maximilian was happy. Then, the current of the bubbling brook increased as the winds picked up. Pine cones blew through the underbrush. The clouds thickened and the sky darkened. Maximilian drew his vest tight and took shelter under a thistle bush at the base of a sturdy spruce tree.

The heavens opened. Trails of lightning traced through the sky, like the gnashing of angry teeth. It was not raining, but Maximilian felt drenched with his own sweat. He was becoming more and more afraid.

In the distance, Maximilian could hear a sound building. He felt it was bearing down on top of him.

Suddenly, Maximilian saw the curve of a steel plow. A mighty bulldozer burst through the bushes and shrubbery. It destroyed everything in its path. Now, the old oak tree that Maximilian's family called home lay directly in its path . . .

Maximilian woke up feeling sick to his stomach. He fumbled for the latch of the portal hatch and forced it open. The air was by no means refreshing, but it was better than the air inside the time machine.

Maximilian climbed to the ground. He was soaked with sweat. He shook his fur dry and realized how dusty and filthy his clothes were. How nice it would be to finally be back home, to take a bath, and to have a change of clothes.

Maximilian noticed that it was quieter in the boat than it had been before. He flipped his pocket watch open and made out two o'clock in the darkness. Maximilian was not tired anymore. It was early morning and he was hungry.

He thought back to the crate of potatoes and turnips he had hid in earlier. He wondered what other foods had been stowed away on the ship. Surely its passengers would be asleep by now. This might be the safest time for him to search for food.

Maximilian crept along carefully. He tried to keep track of his movements so he could find his way back.

The boat continued to astonish him. It was cramped and dirty. The people onboard had been herded together like cattle. Most of the passengers were fast asleep. It was amazing that any of them could sleep with the hard, stained floorboards as their beds.

Maximilian could not help but think back to those he had met along his trip. All of them, from President Lincoln to Samuel Clemens, had been able to lay their tired heads on soft, clean linens.

What promise had been made to these people for them to endure such hardships? What life was waiting for them at the end of their travels?

It must be a wonderful life indeed, Maximilian thought. Then he saw her. In the middle of all of these people lay the young girl Maximilian had seen crying. She lay with her head on her father's chest and her coat serving as her blanket. She seemed peaceful.

Surely these people brought food with them, Maximilian thought. He inched closer to the girl. Maximilian made his way ever so slightly toward the girl's coat pocket. Her green eyes were closed, but Maximilian could imagine them flipping open at any moment.

His nose detected something in her pocket. His head warned him to be careful, but his stomach urged him to go farther.

He crawled on his belly, holding his breath as he went into the coat pocket. His senses had not misled him. Next to a scrap of paper and a small polished stone, Maximilian found a small piece of corn bread. Although stale, it tasted like pure heaven.

Immediately Maximilian felt a rush of energy. It was time for him to find his way back to the time machine.

Maximilian cautiously stuck his nose out of the pocket. He took two healthy whiffs of his surroundings. His whiskers detected nothing of immediate threat.

Maximilian stepped out of the pocket and brushed a few stray crumbs from his fur. He turned to make his way to the floor, but froze. He found himself staring directly into two large, green eyes!

Chapter 5:
ASHLING

The girl was surprised to find the gray field mouse she had seen earlier shaking with fear on her coat pocket.

"Please, don't be afraid," the girl said in a soft voice.

She moved her hand carefully past him and into her pocket.

"I see you already found the corn bread I saved for you," she said. A smile crept onto her face.

Maximilian was hesitant. His mother had taught him from a very young age that humans were not to be trusted.

"Please, don't be afraid," she repeated. Maximilian knew she must be able to see how frightened he was.

"I was hoping you would come back," the girl continued. "I had never seen a mouse quite like you before. You were a nice distraction from everything that has happened these last few days."

It was still very dark in the boat, but the pain in this girl's eyes was very clear. He had been so distracted by her eyes that he had not noticed her freckles. The brilliant red hair she wore up earlier was now free flowing.

"I have not made any friends on this trip," the girl continued in a whisper. "I was hoping you might be my first."

Maximilian's muscles eased slightly. Maybe it was her tone more than her words that made him trust her. Maximilian managed a smile. This delighted the girl. She opened a delicate hand to him.

He had made it this far on his journey by following his **instincts**. Most of the people and animals had not made him regret his decisions. Maximilian took a leap of faith and stepped warily into the girl's palm.

"I don't know about you, my little mouse, but I could certainly use some fresh air," the girl said. Maximilian nodded in agreement.

The girl got to her feet and stepped over the sleeping families. She handled Maximilian very carefully. Her gentle touch was reassuring to him.

A lone doorway led to the upper levels of the ship. They climbed the wooden stairway. Opening the door, they stepped out onto the boat's deck and into the cool, crisp night air.

It did not take long for Maximilian to forget the warm quarters below. The frosty chill nipped at his whiskers and tail.

The girl placed Maximilian carefully on an air vent so that she could put her coat on. Maximilian took the time to unroll his shirt sleeves and cinch his vest closed. For a moment, he contemplated running away from her and hiding again. Something, however, convinced him to stay.

Maximilian could see the girl's breath in the air. The clear night sky was blanketed with stars. The last time he had seen a sky so beautiful he was on the plains of Utah with a blonde prairie dog named Madeline. That thought alone warmed him.

The girl, her red hair blowing in the winds, buttoned her simple blue coat. She blew air into her cupped hands.

Maximilian watched a large, white pelican that was perched on the far railing. The pelican was a very **regal** bird. His deep, bowl-shaped mouth impressed Maximilian. His brilliant white feathers were **silhouetted** against the dark night sky.

The pelican made eye contact with Maximilian and nodded at him. Maximilian felt honored that the bird had recognized him. He returned the nod with a dip of his own head.

"Are you too cold?" the girl asked. He shook his head. Right then, he decided that he would only use head nods and hand gestures with her.

Maximilian watched her as she looked out over the calm water. They were alone.

The boat was a steamship. Two large, black smokestacks billowed steam high into the sky. The boat moved efficiently through the water.

"My name is Ashling," the girl said, looking at him. Maximilian looked back with surprise. He had never heard that name before, but it had a noble sound to it and he liked it. Even on the deck in the pre-dawn hours, Maximilian could see that the girl was blushing at his expression.

"I know it's a strange name," she said, embarrassed. "Father says that it means 'a vision' or 'a dream.' He says that he and mother knew right away that it was what they wished to name me when I was born. At first sight, I was a dream to behold."

Maximilian liked the girl's name and the story behind it. "Ashling," he said quietly to himself in the stillness of the night.

Chapter 6:
A SAD STORY

The bright moon and tiny stars lit the calm ocean waters. Finally, a man revealed himself at one end of the boat. He eyed Ashling for a brief moment before continuing down the deck. He checked riggings and cables as he went.

"I'm sorry you saw me crying earlier," Ashling said. "I didn't think anyone was around."

Maximilian stayed mute. He tried to tell the girl that there was no need to apologize with a look.

"This has been such a long and difficult journey," she continued. "I'd held those emotions in since we left Dublin."

Maximilian could see tears welling in her eyes again. For the first time, he also detected a very strong accent in her voice. It was like nothing he had heard before.

"It feels good to have someone to talk to," Ashling said. She looked at Maximilian curled up on the air duct. "Even if you don't understand me, it's comforting just to get some of what I've been feeling out in the open."

She blew air into her hands again.

"Do you understand me, little one?" she asked, not expecting a response. She smiled at him.

"Father has worked so hard ever since Jonathan and I were born. The decision to leave everything for a strange land could not have been an easy one," Ashling said, placing her hands in her pockets.

She sat on a nearby storage bench, her head now inches from Maximilian.

"I do not know where it is you call home," she continued, "maybe this boat, but my family had lived in Ireland for many, many years."

If she only knew, Maximilian thought.

"Each year there were fewer and fewer crops. It became more and more difficult for

Father to provide for us," Ashling said. "It didn't seem to matter how hard or how long he worked, the potatoes and the money were just not there."

She took a handkerchief from her pocket and dried her eyes. Maximilian wrapped his long tail around himself as the cold night air settled into his bones. He almost wished they would go back below deck.

"I can still remember that day as though it were yesterday," she continued. "The landlord came and told Father that we had lost the land and the house. We had nowhere to go. We had no other choice but to give up everything we had ever known."

Upon hearing this, Maximilian forgot the cold chill that had taken hold of him. This girl's story, the story of her family, was not like his, it *was* his! Sitting right here in front of him was a girl who knew almost exactly how he felt. Her pain was what he struggled with every time he climbed into the time machine.

Maximilian took two strides closer to the girl. He carefully reached his paw out and

placed it on her shoulder. The look on her face
as he did was truly priceless. The grief in her
eyes lessened and she smiled at him again.

So many animals had shown him kindness
on his trip. It was time he returned the favor.

Chapter 7:
A BRIGHT HOPE

Ashling slowly reached into her other coat pocket. She removed a corner of a saltine cracker.

"I was saving this for later, but would you like to have it?" she asked as she placed it on the vent next to him. Maximilian felt almost guilty taking it, but he did not know when his next meal would be. He lowered his head and began to nibble on its edges. As he did, Ashling continued her story.

"We packed whatever we could and decided to spend whatever money we had left on coming to America," she said. Maximilian's ears perked up.

"It took all of my family's savings to buy the four tickets to make the trip across the Atlantic Ocean," Ashling continued. The sadness in her voice was starting to fade.

"We've heard grand stories of America," Ashling said, staring out at the sea. "The roads are paved with gold! And there's a job on every street corner," she said. Maximilian smiled between bites. He was relieved to hear hope return to her voice.

"When we arrived at the port in Dublin and got on board, we realized our story was not **unique**," Ashling said. She was happy to see Maximilian had finished his cracker.

"There were so many other families, so many other dreams of starting over," she said. "Turns out that many Irish families had lost their land to landlords. In fact, most of the land in Ireland is owned by wealthy landlords back in England," she stated. "That was something I never realized before."

Maximilian followed Ashling's stare to a pair of flags on the ship gently blowing in the breeze. The first was basic and had only green, white, and orange. The second was one that Maximilian recognized. It had the red, white, and blue stars and stripes of the United States.

He closed his eyes and prayed that the country he had learned so much about could deliver on the promises it had made to Ashling and her family.

It was still dark out, but it was nearing dawn. Ashling continued with her story.

"Our small farm was located outside the village of Shannon," Ashling began again. "A man by the name of Cooper had leased it to my parents well before I was born.

"Shannon was a splendid place to grow up!" Ashling said, her eyes brightening. "The greenest grass you have ever seen—like a beautiful emerald!"

Maximilian smiled. He certainly knew what it was like to grow up in a place so special. Hearing Ashling talk about Shannon was like hearing him speak about Tanner's Glen.

"I never took our home for granted," Ashling said. "We were not a wealthy family, but my parents made sure we did not go without." She stared out at the open water.

Maximilian nodded at Ashling. Shannon sounded like a fine place to live.

A loud blast from the steam whistle startled both of them. It was followed by a dark stream of smoke swelling from one of the smokestacks. Maximilian traced the smoke's path through the sky. High above, he noticed for the first time that a crewman was perched in a **crow's nest** high above the boat's deck.

Ashling sat on her hands in an attempt to warm them. "Father had grown potatoes on Mr. Cooper's land from the very beginning," she said. "Even after the Great Potato Famine in 1842, the potato continued to be the major crop in Ireland. It wasn't easy after the **blight**, but Father had always made it work."

Her eyes closed slowly. Maximilian knew that look all too well. He imagined she was picturing her home back in Shannon—a home she might never see again.

Maximilian sat on the air vent and drew his knees up toward his chest. A warm beam of sunlight was beginning to rise above the eastern horizon.

"I'm sure New York City will be kind to my family just like Ireland was," Ashling whispered. "As long as we're all together." She turned to face Maximilian. Her cheeks looked cold as the wind blew through her brilliant red hair.

"I appreciate you being a fine gentleman and listening to all of my problems," Ashling said. She again opened her hand and placed it in front of him. It was warm from having been under her leg. That warmth felt good on the bottom of Maximilian's feet as he stepped carefully into her palm.

"We should probably go back downstairs, my friend," she whispered to him. "Father and Mother might be worried if they wake to find me gone."

She was very gentle with him as they crossed the **starboard** bow of the ship. They climbed back downstairs into the cargo hold of the boat.

It was dark and stuffy in the bottom of the ship. Maximilian wondered how long they had been at sea and how much longer they had to go to reach New York.

Ashling's story had reminded Maximilian of his stop in Utah in the time machine. Like the Franklins and the other **pioneers** traveling westward, they were gambling on a better life waiting for them at the end of their voyage.

Ashling settled in next to her parents and her brother, who were still sleeping soundly on the hard floor. She placed Maximilian next to her and looked at him. He waited until she closed her eyes to return to the time machine.

It was harder than he had thought to find his way back through the maze of boxes and crates. But before too long he was back inside the time portal. Maximilian decided to write in his journal to pass the time.

He ran his paw over the leather cover and turned to an empty page. Putting pencil to paper, he began to write.

Chapter 8:
FOLLOW
DIRECTIONS

Maximilian was jarred by noise in the hold. He had written long into the morning inside the time machine. He had thought long and hard about where he was, where he was going, and whether or not he would succeed on his quest.

Now, Maximilian heard voices. There was more stirring amongst the passengers than yesterday. It felt as if the steamer was going much slower than before.

"We will be pulling into New York Harbor within the hour. It is important that you follow directions when we arrive," a strong, booming voice instructed. "Do exactly what you are told when we arrive in New York," the man repeated.

"What about our things?" a voice asked. "What shall we do with our things?"

This question set off a series of side conversations. The instructor hushed them rather than trying to speak over them.

"Your things will stay on the boat," he yelled. "The ship itself will dock and remain in **quarantine** for twenty-four hours. It is the United States **Customs** policy," he informed them.

Another wave of noise swept through the weary travelers.

"I can assure you nothing will happen to your belongings," the man promised them. "The American War Department will keep a watchful eye on all the ships in the harbor." This did little to calm their nerves.

Maximilian was relieved to hear that the luggage would remain on the boat. The quarantine would allow the time machine's battery to recharge.

Knowing the time machine would be secure for a while, he jumped from the cockpit.

Maximilian raced to see Ashling, sure that she would be scared.

Maximilian found Ashling. If she was nervous, she was doing a good job of hiding it from her parents and younger brother. In fact, she knelt beside her brother, reassuring him that everything would be fine. Maximilian continued to be impressed by her strength.

The man giving instructions had also passed out papers to the passengers. They were written in a number of different languages including English. The **immigrants** who could read took their time to scan the information. Then, they discussed it amongst themselves.

Maximilian kept his eyes squarely on Ashling.

"It will be alright, Jonathan," she said. "We need to be strong for Father and Mother."

The small boy looked at his feet. The hat he wore shielded his face from view.

"It says here that we will be brought to a place called Ellis Island," Ashling's father informed her mother. "They will put us through tests before we are allowed to enter the country."

Suddenly, a small, burly man spoke to the entire crowd from the ladder that led to the upper deck. "Come, everyone!" he yelled in his best broken English. "We're coming in New York Harbor! It is a glorious sight to behold!"

Several people immediately rushed up the stairs. The elderly and those who appeared especially weak and tired took their time.

Ashling saw Maximilian and her face brightened. She motioned to him. He was excited to see New York City, too. And he felt safe when he was with her.

Maximilian ran to her. She scooped him up and into her coat pocket in a single motion.

"Thank you so much for coming back," Ashling said, peering into her pocket at him. "Now, let's go see what all the fuss is about, shall we?" she said. Then, she followed her family toward the ladder.

Chapter 9:
LADY LIBERTY

They climbed the stairs into the bright morning sunlight. Maximilian dug his nails into the material lining and climbed upward so he could see out of the pocket.

The observation deck was much more crowded than it had been in the early morning hours. Ashling was tiny, but she was able to work her way to one of the railings facing north toward the city skyline.

"Oh my," Ashling whispered. Then Maximilian saw what the rest of the boat had already seen. Maximilian's mouth fell open in astonishment. He fought the urge to blink, fearing he might miss something.

"I have dreamed about this moment ever since my father told us we would be making this trip," Ashling said to Maximilian. "I could not have imagined it would be this spectacular."

Maximilian had to agree. Despite being several hundred yards out still, the buildings were huge. They sprang from the ground like the biggest trees he had ever seen. They towered over everything they left behind on the ground. Maximilian managed to swallow hard. He wrapped his tail around himself in a reassuring hug.

The steamship they were on moved through the boats already in New York Harbor. Some people on the ship wept and wiped at their eyes with their shirt sleeves. Others embraced and shared a quiet moment together. Ashling's father placed a hand on her shoulder and she looked up at him. He nodded at her and smiled.

The skyline of New York City represented everything these poor immigrants had dreamed of—hard work, opportunity, new beginnings, and most importantly, hope. Maximilian could not imagine the hustle and bustle that occupied the streets of such a large city.

It felt as though the boat's motor had turned completely off. Its humming sound had given way to the lapping of waves against the boat's side.

Maximilian noticed that many of those on board were reading the papers that had been handed out. Maximilian wondered what exactly the leaflet said. Did it give them the history of New York City? Did it warn them of what dangers lay ahead?

"Oh my, look!" a woman near the bow yelled. She pointed to a spot in front of the boat. As Maximilian's eyes followed her finger, they grew ten times larger and he gasped with surprise.

Maximilian tried to catch his breath. Suddenly, he realized that a teardrop was scrolling down his own face.

A statue of a woman draped in a simple gown stood in New York Harbor, towering over them. She wore a spiked crown and cradled a tablet in one arm. The other arm held a torch. She held the torch straight in the air. She was beautiful.

The statue's face impressed Maximilian the most. The eyes showed love and comfort. He had seen many things on his journey and something about this statue and what she stood for made him weep.

Ashling looked down in her pocket at him.

"Can you see, little one?" she whispered.

Maximilian nodded and smiled. He could see the same emotion in her eyes. The sight of this statue must have been a powerful end to the journey Ashling and her parents had begun weeks earlier.

A man next to them read from the leaflet. He spoke surprisingly clearly considering English seemed to be his second language. Maximilian wondered if the brochure included his native tongue.

"The Statue of Liberty!" he said, looking up at her and squinting into the morning sun. "French sculptor Frederic Auguste Bartholdi was comm . . . **commissioned** to design a sculpture with the year 1876 in mind, to celebrate the **centennial** of the American

Declaration of Independence," the man continued.

By now, all those around the man were listening to him.

"The Statue of Liberty was constructed by both France and the United States," he read. "It was agreed that the Americans would build the pe...**pedestal**. The French people were responsible for the statue and its assembly here in New York."

The steamship had moved closer to the Statue of Liberty. All those on board gazed upward.

A woman spoke in a language Maximilian was unfamiliar with. "What did that woman just say?" another stranger asked, equally confused.

"She said that Alexandre Gustave Eiffel, the designer of the Eiffel Tower in Paris, helped design the metal skeleton and framework. It allows such a huge statue to stand upright," a translator explained. "The woman is from the French countryside. She had heard stories about the Statue of Liberty. It was her dream to see it," another passenger said.

Maximilian strained his eyes as the boat slowly drifted by. He could almost make out the words on Lady Liberty's tablet. The tablet was engraved with the date July 4, 1776 in Roman numerals. That was the day America celebrated its independence from Britain.

The amazement over the Statue of Liberty gave way to a renewed worry over the entry process. To be allowed to stay in this land of opportunity, the immigrants had to pass hours of exams and inspections. Many had made it this far and many more were certain to be turned away.

Ashling slipped her pinky finger inside the pocket next to Maximilian.

"I'm nervous," she said in a low voice.

Maximilian took her finger in his paws and held it firm. He was nervous too.

Chapter 10:
WE MADE IT!

If the boat had carried passengers of a higher status, many would have already been **processed**. The Irish steamship carried only lower class immigrants.

The passengers of this boat would be loaded onto **barges**. These barges would transfer the passengers to immigrant stations located on a small island not far from the Statue of Liberty. The island was called Ellis Island.

Their temporary move from the steamship to Ellis Island would not be considered a legal landing. They were still on a ship and the responsibility of the transportation companies.

Once they docked at Ellis Island, the immigrants would pass through a detailed process of examination. During these tests, information would be collected and recorded as accurately as possible.

There were three main parts to the examination. The first was the medical exam. It would be performed by officers of the Public Health and Marine Hospital Service.

The barge slammed against the supports of the loading ramp. Maximilian saw officers wearing neatly pressed uniforms and identification badges everywhere he looked. The officers were closely watching the weary travelers.

Maximilian could feel Ashling trembling. She held her father's hand tightly as they made their way into a large brick building. Her mother was close behind them holding Jonathan in her arms.

"Stay close, everyone," her father warned. "We cannot get separated here. With all of these people, we very well might not ever see each other again."

Her father was right to caution them. The building they entered emptied into one enormous station. It was divided with ropes and walls into dozens of **cubicles** and lines.

The first exams checked the immigrants for physical weaknesses or diseases. Maximilian had seen that Ashling's brother looked pale. The lack of sunlight, poor nutrition, and exhaustion from the trip were beginning to take their toll.

Before going any farther, Ashling's mother placed him on the ground. She bent in front of him and said, "There you go, Jonathan. It won't be much longer and we'll be able to get you something to eat." The boy stood uneasily on his frail legs.

His mother took his cheeks between her fingers and squeezed them. Jonathan's cheeks turned rosy red and his face took on a healthy glow.

"Good," her father said. He motioned them toward a long, winding line.

"Everyone from the Dublin boat that just docked at Port A, please get into the far left line," a conductor instructed the crowd.

"Here we go," Ashling said to Maximilian. His heart began pounding in his chest. He clutched her finger even tighter than before and sank lower in her pocket so as not to be detected.

Maximilian recognized some of the people in their line from the boat. There was the man who had translated the French woman's information regarding the Statue of Liberty. There was the woman who had cried out when the statue had first come into view.

Many of the people in line looked very similar to Ashling's family. They were tired and hungry. Their clothes were tattered and worn. There were also many others who looked far worse off. Maximilian wondered what their chances were of gaining access into the United States.

Those gathered together on Ellis Island made up a melting pot of **ethnicities**. They reminded Maximilian of just how big the world was beyond the tree lines and green pastures of Tanner's Glen.

Maximilian wondered how many of his own relatives had passed through this very port or one similar to it. Sadly, he knew very little of his own family history.

On his mother's side, his ancestors came to Tanner's Glen from countries in Western Europe. They had come with a group seeking the freedom to practice their religion without fear. His great-great-grandfather Monroe J. Mouse and his wife, Anne, had made the passage with a group of **Pilgrims**. They came on a ship called the *Mayflower*. Maximilian knew very little else about them.

Maximilian's watch chimed noon. For the first time in a while, he was reminded of his own journey. The health exam that Ashling and her family were about to take would determine his own fate. He needed everyone in her family to pass these tests in order to be allowed back on their ship to get their bags. There the time machine would be waiting patiently for him.

"Next!" another short, middle-aged man barked. Ashling's father stepped forward holding Ashling's hand. A woman dressed in a nursing uniform stood next to the officer. On the officer's shoulders were gold striped patches. They were similar to patches worn by the officers that Maximilian had seen in attendance at President Lincoln's Gettysburg Address.

Are these military officers? Maximilian wondered before climbing deeper into Ashling's pocket. He most certainly did not want to be found and become the reason she was not allowed into the United States.

"Are these other three all with you?" the officer asked, eyeing them from head to toe.

"Yes, sir," Ashling's father responded.

"Your papers, please," the officer said. He motioned them to step to the side of the line.

The officer placed his glasses on and began flipping through the papers. At the same time, the nurse began checking Ashling, Jonathan, and her mother for illness.

First, she checked their eyes. Then, she had them open their mouths so she could examine their teeth and tongue. Next, they rolled up their sleeves to be examined for skin rashes. Finally, she looked in their ears and examined their postures.

The nurse said very little. She just gave specific instructions on what to do and how to stand. Maximilian took this to be a good sign. If she had any concerns, chances were she would have voiced them to the officer.

"It says here you are from Shannon, Ireland," the officer said. "What are your plans if you are admitted into the United States?" he asked.

"My plans, sir?" Ashling's father asked.

"Yes, what do you plan on doing for a living? How will you support your family?" the officer said in a stern and annoyed voice.

"Well, I farmed my entire life. I hope to do the same here," Ashling's father explained. "I have heard the land in the West is some of the best in the world," he said.

The officer stamped the papers and handed them back to Ashling's father.

"Next!" the officer yelled. Ashling and her family, along with Maximilian, were hustled through to the next checkpoint.

Maximilian's heart slowed for a moment and he was again able to breathe. It was hot in Ashling's pocket, but most of his sweat came from his nerves. She opened the pocket so that Maximilian could get some fresh air.

"We made it!" she said with excitement. She didn't know that they would have two more exams. They had to pass those as well before being allowed through to the city.

Maximilian breathed a heavy sigh of relief and drank in the rush of refreshing air. He gave Ashling a wink, which she returned with a smile.

"You're going to make it," Maximilian said to himself. "We're going to make it."

Chapter 11:
I'LL DO ANYTHING

The immigrants who passed the first exam were hustled through the bustling main detention center at Ellis Island. Maximilian peeked out over the edge of the pocket. He could hear the different languages being spoken amongst people finding their line and organizing the necessary paperwork.

"How are you holding up, Mr. Mouse?" Ashling asked in concern. It was amazing that despite all that she was going through, she was worried about his well-being. She was a strong girl, indeed.

Sunlight poured through the high, arching windows that decorated the impressive brick building. It lay like a blanket over those that had gathered on the island.

"Over here," Ashling's father instructed. He pointed to a second station manned by several more officials dressed in navy blue uniforms.

The station had a **crest** with the slogan *The Empire State* and an American flag. Maximilian was becoming used to seeing the stars and stripes on every stop of his journey in the time machine.

Ashling and Maximilian made their way to the next exam. It would see if immigrants had any nonphysical reasons that might delay their entrance.

Of the three middle-aged men who greeted them, two had their arms crossed. One was seated behind a small wooden desk. The desk had a pile of papers with a list of questions already outlined on them.

The man at the desk did not make eye contact with them as they approached. With his eyes squarely on the list of questions, he began his rehearsed script. The other two men looked suspiciously over the family.

What exactly were they looking for?

Maximilian felt as nervous as he did when he operated the time machine. He had known this young Irish girl for less than twenty-four hours, but she had certainly made a lasting impression on him.

"Where are you from?" the inspector asked.

"Ireland, sir. Shannon, Ireland," Ashling's father said.

The officer, upon hearing this response, made a quick note on the paper.

"How many in your party?" the man continued.

"Four," her father said. "My wife, daughter, the boy, and myself."

"Do you have any relatives already living in the United States of America?" the man asked.

"Yes, my wife's sister," Ashling's father responded. "She lives in the city with her husband."

Maximilian's ears perked up at hearing this surprising answer. Ashling had not mentioned anything about relatives. Surely he was being sincere. Being caught in a lie at this point would harm their chances of being let in.

"Finally," the officer said, "how do you intend to support your family?"

For a brief moment, a strange silence seemed to fill the entire building. Maximilian waited for Ashling's father to answer. He wondered what was taking him so long. It dawned on Maximilian that he was fighting the urge to cry.

"As I told the man at the first station . . . anything," he finally managed. "Anything it takes in order to make sure there's food on the table and a roof over our head." He held his chin high and made direct eye contact with the officials judging him.

The inspector behind the desk looked up from his paperwork at hearing this response. Maximilian thought he even managed a smile.

"Clearly and beyond a doubt entitled to admission into these United States of America?" the man asked aloud, reading from the lower portion of the sheet.

"Yes," he said, answering his own question. He made a large check mark on the paper.

"Welcome to New York City," the inspector said. He pointed to the far end of the building.

"You may proceed to the **discharging** quarters."

Ashling, her parents, and her brother said nothing as they walked to the far door.

Maximilian noticed that throughout the entire line of questioning, Ashling had never let go of her father's firm grasp. This made him smile.

Chapter 12:
NEW DANGERS

Ashling and Maximilian made their way with the others to the discharging quarters. On the way, they passed a rack of newspapers. Ashling's father paused briefly and then stopped. He leaned closer to examine a headline from a paper called the *Chicago Post*. From his hiding place in Ashling's pocket, Maximilian could barely make out the subheading with his keen eyesight:

"The Irish fill our prisons, our poor houses... Scratch a convict or a **pauper***, and the chances are that you tickle the skin of an Irish Catholic. Putting them on a boat and sending them home would end crime in this country."*

Ashling watched as her father straightened and turned to her mother.

"This way," he said without emotion. He led them toward a door that opened into the brilliant New York day.

Once outside, Maximilian glanced nervously around the bay. He searched for the boat they had come in on. Finally it caught his attention. It was anchored not far from the island. He allowed himself a slight feeling of relief.

Outside the processing building, there was a tall, white-haired man dressed all in black with a white collar. He greeted them with a warm smile.

Maximilian recognized him as a priest. He was relieved that he was not another officer. The man really seemed happy to see them.

"Hello," he said in a soft voice. "Welcome to our fair city. My name is Father O'Malley." He extended a hand to them, while embracing a Bible in the other.

As if on command, the family changed. They seemed to transform into more hopeful images of themselves.

"I am a **missionary** with St. Peter and Paul's Parish in lower Manhattan," Father O'Malley continued. He was sure to make eye contact with every one of them.

"I volunteer to greet immigrants like you as they conclude their processing here at Ellis Island," he said. His flowing, shoulder-length white hair immediately reminded Maximilian of Mark Twain, who he had met during his time on the *Mississippi Belle*.

"We are very grateful, Father," Ashling's mother said. "It has been such a long trip. We have not even had time to get our bearings."

"I understand," Father O'Malley replied. "Believe me, many of our Irish brothers and sisters have gone through this process."

"We get the impression that we Irish might have worn out our welcome here," Ashling's father spoke up. He was referring to the story in the newspaper he saw.

"Well, one of the reasons I am here is to educate you on the dangers that exist on the other side of this harbor," the kindhearted priest said. He turned his stare to the city skyline.

"Dangers?" Ashling said uneasily. Maximilian was just beginning to think that the family's luck had turned and that the worst was behind them. A troubled feeling came over him.

"Yes, dangers," Father O'Malley repeated. "Come, let us talk some more."

Chapter 13:
GIVE ME YOUR TIRED . . .

A light, cool breeze blew in off the harbor. It swept into Ashling's pocket and played with the fur on Maximilian's face.

"I did not mean to frighten you fine people," Father O'Malley said, eyeing young Jonathan as he walked. "I cater to everyone who comes in off the boats. But I could tell you and your family were straight from Ireland after seeing the hair on this young lass." His gentle blue eyes fell directly on Ashling, her bright red hair caressed by the blowing wind.

"I have seen so many of our countrymen coming through Ellis Island," Father O'Malley continued as they stopped. He bent to pick up a small wicker basket. "Since the potato famine, Irish immigrants have been coming to

New York in **droves**." He removed the cloth towel draped over the basket and took out two bright red apples.

"I arrived on these shores almost twenty years ago," Father O'Malley said. He handed one of the apples to Jonathan and the other to Ashling. "This city has many opportunities, but many dangers as well."

The priest warned, "Once the ferry drops you off at the east docks, you will be approached by peddlers, beggars, and opportunists."

He handed out apples to both of Ashling's parents. "They usually prey on the immigrants who have no place to stay," Father O'Malley said. "Do you have anyone here you can trust?"

Ashling's father finished chewing a juicy bite of apple. "Yes, fortunately," he managed to say. "My wife's sister lives here with her husband. They've agreed to house us for a short while."

Father O'Malley brought his hands together in a prayer-like pose. "That is fine news . . . fine news indeed," he said. "Many immigrants who have no one to turn to end up in **tenement** houses. Landlords charge an outrageous fee for their services. Most immigrants end up living on the streets as beggars.

"Try not to be discouraged by the storefronts with signs that say 'No Irish Need Apply,'" O'Malley continued, his voice tender. "As long as you are willing to take any job, you can find something," he said. He placed a reassuring hand on Jonathan's head as he spoke.

Maximilian could see the hesitancy building in everyone's face.

"Remember that you will always have the Church to support you," the clergyman said. "You are always welcome in my parish."

Father O'Malley turned to Ashling. "Did you take notice, by chance, of what it said on the Statue of Liberty when you arrived?" he asked.

Ashling shook her head no. Then, she looked back out into the bay at the statue. Father O'Malley knelt on one knee, looking eye-level at the girl's young face.

"It is part of a poem written by Emma Lazarus in 1883 called 'The New Colossus,'" he said. "It had such a powerful effect on me when I came to the United States that I memorized it. It says,

"Give me your tired, your poor, your huddled masses yearning to breathe free. The wretched **refuse** *of your teeming shore. Send these, the homeless,* **tempest**-*tossed to me."*

Father O'Malley handed Ashling another apple.

"Do you understand, child?" he asked her.

"Yes," Ashling said. "I think I do."

Maximilian kept hidden, but he heard every word—and he understood too.

Chapter 14:
NEARLY THROUGH

The kind priest pointed them to the officer responsible for filing their discharge papers. He blessed them and wished them well. Maximilian thought about the warning he had given them.

Maximilian was a single mouse trying to save his home and family. From what he had gathered, it appeared that most of Ireland had been forced to do the same. Being away from home was not easy, regardless of the situation. This Maximilian knew all too well.

A crowd had gathered outside the main building on Ellis Island at the final stage of the admission process.

"I'll wait in line," Ashling's father said to his wife. "Why don't you and the children wait off to the side?" Her mother nodded and led Ashling and Jonathan to a shaded bench under a large maple tree.

It was nice for everyone, including Maximilian, to take a break from the afternoon heat. Ashling reached carefully inside her pocket and Maximilian climbed into her hand. She turned her back on her mother and brother and lifted him to eye level.

"How are you holding up?" she said quietly. Maximilian responded with a reassuring nod. The truth was he was very hot and thirsty.

"I had not mentioned my Auntie Erin to you on the boat," Ashling said, glancing over her shoulder. Jonathan was busy working on his second apple, while her mother rested her eyes.

"I have never met my aunt," she continued. "She moved to the United States shortly after I was born." Maximilian listened closely, happy to have been removed from the stuffy pocket.

"I have heard many stories about her though," Ashling said with excitement. "She and my mother have written letters. I simply cannot wait to meet her!"

Ashling placed Maximilian gently on a nearby stone wall and removed her own coat. She swept several stray locks of hair from her eyes and leaned closer to him.

"My auntie married a serviceman from New York. He had been stationed in Ireland before the great war in Europe," she said. She placed her hands between her knees. "Mother says that he was an officer in the US Navy and that their home here in the city is sure to be grand!"

Maximilian was excited for Ashling.

"Mother also says that Auntie Erin is a very **liberated** woman," Ashling said with a smile reaching from ear to ear. "Much more than women are allowed to be back home. She even started her own seamstress company and helps to support the family!"

Maximilian noticed that Ashling's father had made progress in line. He was nearing his turn to complete the family's papers. At that moment, his pocket watch chimed one.

The family bond he witnessed with Ashling, her parents, and her brother made him long to be home. It also pained him that his own father would not be waiting for him when he eventually returned to the old oak tree.

Then, unexpectedly, another thought crept into his mind. It was a concern he had not had since first arriving on the ship. But it now made the coarse fur on the back of his neck stand on end.

The exterior shell of the time machine had been damaged. There was no guarantee the shell could still protect him from the intense heat of time travel.

Would he ever make it home?

Chapter 15:
GONE!

Maximilian could see Ashling's father talking with the processing officer. His hand gestures suggested that maybe his thick Irish accent was making communication difficult.

Maximilian looked toward the city skyline. A bustling city awaited the Irish family. The city docks were alive with trade. Numerous tugboats and steamships churned their way near the unloading ports. They moved around one another with little room for error.

Whitecaps rolled through the harbor as the breeze stiffened. Some of the smaller ships on the water were tossed over the rolling waves. They came dangerously close to tipping over.

Ashling's father was making his way back to the family. His long stride made him look tall and lean. He clutched several papers tightly in his hand. He seemed to have an added spring in his step as he neared them.

"Well," he said with a large grin, "I guess we should start to think about what we want to do first when we get to New York City."

Ashling squealed with excitement and ran to him. She gave her father a hug. Maximilian watched as tears filled her mother's eyes. She pulled Jonathan close to her and kissed his forehead. For a moment, the family seemed unaware that they were surrounded by thousands of strangers.

"I have never been happier," Ashling said to her parents. She gave her little brother a warm embrace as well. Suddenly she remembered her little friend, waiting patiently for her on the stone hedge.

Ashling walked toward Maximilian. He was happy for her. Her journey was really just beginning.

"I know that look," she said to Maximilian. "But you can come with us, you know. I wish you would come with us."

Maximilian shook his head and she smiled.

"I know," Ashling said sadly. "I figured that is what you would say. But I thought I would make the offer anyway." She sat on the bench next to him.

"I'm not sure if I would have been strong enough to make it through all of this without you, my brave little mouse," Ashling said to Maximilian. "I needed to be strong for my family . . . and you were strong for me." Maximilian only looked at her.

"I have something I wish to give to you for your friendship," Ashling said. She reached inside her coat pocket and produced a small four-leaf clover. She handed it to Maximilian by its stem.

It was so delicate that simply taking it from her worried him. He held it tightly to his chest, touched by her thoughtful gesture. In all his time in Tanner's Glen, Maximilian had never seen a four-leaf clover before.

Maximilian saw a tear roll down Ashling's freckled cheek. She blew him a kiss and turned to walk back to her parents.

"You were strong enough on your own," Maximilian said, louder than he had wanted. It was just loud enough that Ashling spun around to face him.

"I knew you were holding out on me!" she said with amusement. "I knew you could talk and were just being a good listener."

"You were strong enough without me," Maximilian repeated. "I know all of your dreams will come true in the United States."

Ashling said nothing. She simply stood looking at Maximilian.

"I should be going, my friend," she said in her Irish accent. "We have to take the ferry over to the loading docks. The boat we arrived on just left and will meet us there in the morning with our things."

Maximilian looked over the top of Ashling's shoe into the harbor behind her. He could not see the boat that held the time machine! Carefully folding the clover, he placed it safely inside his shirt.

Maximilian ran as hard and as fast as he could toward the pier at the front of Ellis Island. He stopped only for a brief moment to look back at Ashling. She waved good-bye to him.

Panic overtook him and he sprinted toward the wharf. His heart was pounding. He could think of nothing other than finding the boat.

He had gone through so much to get this far. Failure at this point was not an option.

Maximilian arrived at the pier and stopped. He bent at his waist and put his paws on his knees. Trying to catch his breath, he watched as newly arriving passengers from other boats were herded into the large brick building.

"It's over," Maximilian said in frustration. "It's over." The boat was gone.

Chapter 16:
A NEW FRIEND

The heavy rope that had held their boat to the dock hung loosely in the water. Maximilian sat on the side wall and let his legs dangle over the edge.

It was not long ago that Maximilian would have given in and cried in his frustration. He did not cry. He would not allow himself to cry. His cheeks burned and he clenched his jaw tightly to control his feelings.

There had to be a plan. There had to be a way to get from Ellis Island to the boatyard where his boat was headed.

Maximilian knew he had until tomorrow morning. The crew would begin unloading the cargo then. If he did not develop a plan to get to the boat before then, the time machine would most certainly be destroyed or lost.

There was a lull in the activity at Ellis Island. Maximilian wondered whether or not more boats would arrive to deliver more candidates for entry into New York. For now, however, Maximilian was alone with his thoughts.

Maximilian was distracted by a pair of seagulls hanging on the wind currents above him. He could only guess whether or not they saw him. They appeared more concerned with finding their next clam or oyster.

"Why so glum, chap?" a voice asked. Maximilian turned.

"You certainly look to be down on your luck, if you ask me," a large, white pelican said to him. Maximilian immediately recognized him. He had looked so impressive perched on the boat railing, looking out over the open water.

So much had happened since he and Ashling had sat in the cool, night air talking. Now, they were realizing their dream and would be resting comfortably in the home of relatives before nightfall.

"The boat that we arrived on," Maximilian said, looking at the pelican who had inched closer to him. "I expected it to still be here."

The bird cocked his head and looked at Maximilian. "The boat will be taken somewhere else to wait out the remaining time on its quarantine," he explained. "It's too busy to stay docked here. More boats will be arriving shortly."

That's what Maximilian was afraid of. Who knew where the boat was now and if Maximilian would ever be able to locate it?

"You know," the pelican went on, "it's too bad that field mice are not able to fly."

This remark caught Maximilian off guard. *What an odd thing to say,* he thought.

"That is a shame," Maximilian replied as he turned away.

"Surely, I jest," the pelican said. "You'll have to excuse me. I'm British, you see, and we're not known for our humor."

Maximilian smiled.

"My apologies," the pelican said again. "Allow me to make it up to you."

Maximilian heard these words in between several blasts of an air horn. He turned to watch a large liner make its way past Ellis Island toward the open water.

"I would certainly appreciate any help you could give me," Maximilian said with renewed hope.

"Very good!" the pelican exclaimed, "very good indeed!"

Chapter 17:
FASTER . . .

"You would be willing to help me?" Maximilian asked. He was impressed with the bird's generosity. "I don't even know your name," he said.

"The name is Patton van Pelican. I am a proud member of Her Majesty's Royal Bird Force," the pelican said with a wink and a swell of his chest. "The Royal Bird Force has been serving mother England for centuries. It is made of birds like myself, as well as messenger pigeons and hawks."

Maximilian was impressed. He had known right away, when he had first seen Patton, that he was **distinguished**.

"It is so nice to meet you, Patton," Maximilian said. "My name is Maximilian P. Mouse, and I would certainly like to hear your plan," he said.

"Truth be told," Patton started, "I have absolutely no idea where your particular boat went off to." He said this in a way that gave Maximilian no sign that he was worried about this fact.

"So," Maximilian asked with concern, "where do you suggest we go from here?"

Patton chuckled and pointed upward with a fan of his wing. "Why up, of course!" he said with an inspired tone. "It would certainly help our cause if we were to get a bird's-eye view of the situation, don't you think, Maximilian?" Patton joked.

Maximilian laughed, although he was scared of flying. He had never flown before in his life. He honestly knew of no one in his species that had.

Patton took a minute to reach inside the heavier layer of his feathers. He rummaged through his down as if he were itching himself. Suddenly, he produced a small pair of goggles.

"These might just work," Patton proclaimed proudly. "Here, my good fellow, give these a

try, won't you? I wear these in bad weather and they might just fit you."

Maximilian humored Patton and strapped the foam-padded goggles around his head. They slipped down his nose at first, but after he adjusted the worn leather strap, they actually fit quite well.

"Just one more thing," Patton said. He cleaned the lenses with a wing feather. "There, now you are officially ready to go flying!" he declared.

Maximilian's feet tingled and his stomach felt woozy. "Are you sure about this?" he asked, a hint of doubt in his voice. "Have you ever flown with someone on your back before?" Maximilian asked.

"My fine fellow, you have absolutely nothing to worry about," Patton said reassuringly. "I am one of the most decorated pelicans, nay birds, to ever fly for the crown."

Patton could tell that Maximilian was worried by the look in his eyes. He took one step closer to Maximilian with a large, webbed foot and gently placed a wing on his shoulder.

"Let's go flying, shall we?" he said. Something in his voice convinced Maximilian.

Maximilian nodded. He used the yellow, webbed foot to hoist himself into the small of Patton's back. He sank into the soft, velvety feathers between the pelican's shoulder blades.

"Take hold of my feathers and brace yourself," Patton instructed. "If at any point you need something, simply call out and I'll hear you."

Maximilian gripped a pawful of feathers. He could only manage a firm pat on the bird's back in response to his directions.

"Now," Patton began, "if there is nothing we are forgetting, I would like to welcome today's passengers and thank you for choosing Royal Air."

While Patton's humor was well-intentioned, Maximilian was paying very little attention to him. He was concentrating too hard on not getting sick or passing out.

"Today's flight is for an undetermined amount of time with a cruising **altitude** of approximately 1,000 feet," Patton said continuing his pre-flight talk.

Maximilian squeezed his eyes shut and held his breath.

Patton wet one of his feathers, held it to the breeze, and began to flap his wings.

Faster . . . faster . . . faster . . .

Maximilian held tight to Patton's feathers, sure that he would pull them out. Before he knew it, they were slowly lifting off of Ellis Island and climbing into the clear blue sky.

Chapter 18:
AN AMAZING RIDE

Maximilian felt a strange sensation in his stomach. It was a weightlessness that he had never experienced before.

Patton flew high into the sky at an angle. The wind blew in Maximilian's face and his goggles stuck tight around his eyes. The sun was bright and he found it difficult determining which end was up. Suddenly Patton banked hard and came around back toward Ellis Island.

"Hang on, chap!" Patton yelled as their speed increased. Maximilian continued to hold as tight as he could, his palms beginning to sweat.

When Patton circled back around, Maximilian could see the large brick station.

For the first time, he realized just how high up they were flying. The building came into focus below them.

Ellis Island was bigger than Maximilian had first thought. He couldn't believe he had been inside it with Ashling and her family.

It was such a clear afternoon. He could make out everything, including the smallest details of the building and landscaping.

Another steamship was circling in the waters before docking. Even at their height, Maximilian could hear the engines flip to reverse. The boat's black smoke rose in their direction. The people making their way ashore looked as small as the black ants on the sandy creek beds in Tanner's Glen.

The entire experience of soaring high above Ellis Island was truly breathtaking. Maximilian could not believe that he was actually flying. His nerves had calmed and he was trying to enjoy every minute of the flight.

"We're hitting a little **turbulence**," Patton shouted over his shoulder in Maximilian's direction. "I'm going to climb a little higher."

Maximilian tried not to let this change in altitude affect him. Instead, he concentrated on the Statue of Liberty as they made their way in her direction.

"She's beautiful!" Maximilian yelled, unable to contain his enthusiasm. She had been impressive from the deck of their boat as they entered New York Harbor. But up close at 1,200 feet in the air, she was simply breathtaking!

Patton said nothing and Maximilian wondered if he had even heard him. He stopped flapping for the moment and they simply glided effortlessly on the wind currents high above Lady Liberty.

Maximilian's heart pounded and his pulse raced. He wished that his mother and sister could see this amazing view. He wanted to remember it forever.

Every detail that he had strained to see that morning from the boat came into sight. Maximilian could see that the statue was much more detailed than he originally saw. The robe sleeve that slumped loosely down her right arm was so detailed that Maximilian wondered how the artist had managed. The crown with its spikes sat perched on her parted hair. For the first time, Maximilian was able to see that she wore sandals on her feet.

"This is the best part of the tour," Patton said, the wind blowing through his ivory feathers. "Heeeeeere we go!" he cried and they began to dive.

"My fellow pilots and I estimated that from torch to base, she must be over 300 feet tall," Patton said.

Maximilian could not believe it. Patton came in low and close, circling Lady Liberty's torch. They flew so low at one point, tourists on the ground taking in the view actually paused to point in their direction.

After a number of trips around the statue, Patton began to climb again. He gave four long, deliberate flaps of his wings, moving them forward with ease.

"I wanted you to experience that, my friend," Patton said. Maximilian patted his back with thanks.

"It is the most beautiful thing my eyes have ever seen," Maximilian said. And he meant every word.

"Now," Patton said, "what do you say we find that boat you were looking for, shall we?"

He flew in the direction of downtown New York. The water beneath them looked like glass and it stretched all the way to the horizon.

Somewhere, Maximilian thought, *in that endless stretch of land and water was his home.*

And he would find it.

Chapter 19:
SMOOTH LANDING

Maximilian could hear the faint ring of his pocket watch as the wind whipped through his fur. It was already two o'clock. If Patton could locate the boat, Maximilian could depart on the time machine.

"The part of the city at the very tip of the peninsula is called Manhattan," Patton informed him. "It was originally land that belonged to natives. Later, it was purchased by Dutch settlers," he said, giving Maximilian a brief lesson on New York City history.

The sky was still cloudless, but a front could be seen moving in the far distance. Maximilian wanted to find the boat and make sure everything was right with the time machine.

Patton made a slight change in his course. He headed north up the coast of Manhattan, over some of the busier parts of the city.

Maximilian could tell that Patton was concentrating hard on this portion of the flight. The traffic in the sky had picked up considerably.

"Keep a sharp eye out below for your boat," Patton said. Maximilian was already looking

at the boatyards, sure that he would find the old Irish steamer.

A huge, three-mast clipper ship had just made its way into the harbor. It blocked Maximilian's view with its large sails. Finally, it moved away from the loading docks. That was when Maximilian caught sight of their boat. The green, white, and orange flag still flew proudly over the stern. Its hold was green, the paint chipping.

"That's it! That's it!" Maximilian shouted. He pulled up on Patton's feathers.

"Roger that," Patton said in a formal, military tone. He began to dive.

Maximilian's stomach sank. He barely noticed, however, as excitement and relief took hold of him.

The boat was quiet as it waited for the quarantine to be lifted. Maximilian watched as the deck, the air vents, and the smokestacks got bigger and bigger.

Finally, Patton pulled up with his wings. He brought his feet beneath him for landing. As smoothly as they had taken off at Ellis Island, Patton was returning Maximilian to the ship.

Patton gently touched down on the rear deck. Maximilian jumped to the floor. He removed the goggles and ran a paw through the fur on his head. His tail hung loosely behind him.

"That was truly remarkable," Maximilian said. "I don't know how I possibly could have managed without your help."

Patton was busy stretching. Maximilian watched and wondered if he had heard anything he had said.

"Maximilian, it was my pleasure," Patton finally said. "When I joined the ranks of the Royal Bird Force, I took an oath to serve and protect those who needed help. I have to admit," Patton said, turning to face Maximilian, "that did go better than I had expected. It was the first time I had ever flown with a passenger on my back."

Maximilian looked at him with a blank stare. Patton smiled and gave him a sly wink.

Chapter 20:
TIME TO WRITE

Maximilian climbed back through the wooden hatch that led inside the ship. It was **eerily** quiet. The only sounds were the occasional creaking of the ship as it rocked in the water.

The air was even staler than he had remembered. There was almost no light at all in the hold of the ship. A heavy dust hung in the air.

Maximilian made his way through the chests and crates back to where the time machine had landed. Some of the cargo that did not belong to the passengers had been unloaded, so the path back to the time machine had been slightly different.

Maximilian reminded himself that he was in no hurry. Finally, after a series of wrong turns, he was relieved to find the time machine exactly where he had left it.

Maximilian carefully undid the restraints and opened the portal. He looked at the remaining trunks packed in the bow of the ship. The stamps on the luggage read like a map of Europe from countries like Poland, Italy, Portugal, and Greece.

He had just about an hour to spare before the time machine would be fully charged for his trip to Tanner's Glen. Climbing in the stuffy portal, he grabbed his journal and pencil from his pouch. He turned to the page marked by the red ribbon and saw that he had only a few more pages left to write on.

Like he had so many times before, Maximilian began writing. He tried his hardest to sketch a picture of the Statue of Liberty. He did not want the image he had in his head to ever fade.

The Statue of Liberty represented something different to everyone who saw her guiding light, Maximilian thought. *But she also represented the chance for a better life. She stood tall for those who had been* **persecuted** *in their previous homes. She welcomed them when others had turned them away.*

Maximilian felt proud to have shared in Ashling's experience here on Ellis Island.

Chapter 21:
ANOTHER TRY

Maximilian glanced at his watch and gathered his things. He was getting that familiar feeling in his stomach again. He willed himself to not even think about the crack the acorn shell now had.

He carefully placed the four-leaf clover next to his seat in the time machine. He needed all the luck he could get.

Maximilian began his usual routine. He closed the portal latch and fastened his seat belt. He set the date and destination.

2013, October, 15, Tanner's Glen.

"Hang on, chap," he said to himself, repeating the phrase Patton had used before takeoff.

The time machine sprang to life and began to spin. It seemed to be operating exactly like always. The shell's crack had no effect on the temperature inside the capsule. Maximilian controlled his breathing as the spinning finally began to slow.

His body ached as he removed the seat belt and stretched. He breathed a heavy sigh of relief that Nathaniel's invention had survived the slight crack and that he was okay.

Maximilian pulled out his handkerchief and unlatched the portal lock. The door swung open and he climbed out.

"Please," Maximilian said to himself. "Please let me be in Tanner's Glen."

Maximilian jumped to the ground and immediately felt a sense of dread. His soft pink paws landed on smooth, polished marble. He stood in the shadow of something large, the time machine cooling behind him.

Maximilian rubbed his eyes and stared at the ground. Not only was the ground made of marble, but the walls around him seemed to be as well.

Maximilian skirted the marble base, careful to keep his back close to the wall. He left the shadows and walked into soft moonlight. He saw several amazingly tall pillars at the mouth of the building he was in. This building did not look like anything he had ever seen before.

The pillars towered over him. They were definitely not anywhere near the height of the Statue of Liberty. But they were taller than any of the trees in his forest back home. Unfortunately though, these were not trees, and this was not his forest.

Maximilian slowly turned to see what the marble base supported. His jaw dropped. His paw went to his open mouth. Before him was a gigantic statue of a man seated in a chair. This grand theater housed a statue in honor of President Abraham Lincoln.

About Ellis Island

Between 1892 and 1954, the small island of Ellis Island welcomed immigrants entering the United States. Its spot in New York Harbor was the processing center for more than 12 million immigrants.

The immigrants who went through Ellis Island were looking to improve their lives. They were leaving behind poverty, famine, and religious intolerance. New York City and America represented opportunity, freedom, and hope.

The immigrants came from nations such as Ireland, England, Germany, and Italy. They faced physical examinations and interviews to determine whether or not they would be allowed acceptance into the United States.

The experience was upsetting and tiring. But, it was the last step for those desperate enough to make the dangerous journey.

The success of the United States in the early 1900s drew immigrants from all over the world. They were also drawn to the Statue of Liberty that welcomed them at their arrival.

Some immigrants entered the nation through Boston, Philadelphia, and Baltimore. However, Ellis Island continued to be the entrance for the majority of "huddled masses yearning to breathe free."

Glossary

altitude - the height of something above sea level or ground level.

barge - a large boat with a flat bottom.

blight - a disease or injury of plants.

centennial - a 100-year anniversary.

commission - a request to complete a job or mission.

compliment - a feeling or expression of praise or liking for something.

crest - a symbol or coat of arms for a family or a group.

crow's nest - a platform at the top of a ship's mast. A crow's nest is partly covered and used as a lookout.

cubicle - a small space.

customs - duties or taxes charged on imports or exports for a country.

dapper - very stylish.

discharge - to be released to go.

distinguished - celebrated.

downtrodden - suffering from being held back.

droves - a large number of people.

eerie - strange or creepy.

ethnicity - the relation to a group of people based on a common race, nationality, religion, or culture.

heart-wrenching - causing great sadness.

immigrant - a person who enters another country to live.

instinct - natural knowledge of something.

liberated - freed from traditional attitudes.

missionary - a person who spreads a church's religion.

pauper - a very poor person who must live on public money.

pedestal - a base that something sits on.

persecute - to treat someone badly because of his or her origin, religion, or beliefs.

Pilgrims - the people who sailed from England in 1620 and settled in Plymouth Rock, Massachusetts.

pioneer - one of the first people to settle on new land.

processed - a series of actions or steps that lead to an end result.

quarantine - the separation of people from others in order to stop a disease from spreading.

refuse - the worthless part of something.

regal - excellent or magnificent.

silhouette - the outline of a figure or profile.

starboard - the right side of a ship when facing forward.

tempest - a violent storm.

tenement - an apartment building or property that is not clean, safe, or comfortable.

turbulence - shaking or thrashing around.

unique - being the only one of its kind.

wallow - to become or remain helpless.

About the Author

Maximilian P. Mouse, Time Traveler was created by Philip M. Horender. Horender resides in upstate New York with his wife, Erin, and their dog, MoJo.

Horender earned his Bachelor of Arts in History with a minor in education from St. Lawrence University. He later obtained his Masters in Science in Education from the University at Albany, the State University of New York.

He currently teaches high school history, coaches swimming, and advises his school's history club. When he is not writing, Horender enjoys biking, kayaking, and hiking with Erin and MoJo.